CHRISTMAS CRISIS!

Illustrated by Woody Fox

RED FOX

CHRISTMAS CRISIS!
A RED FOX BOOK 978 1 862 30886 2

First published in Great Britain by Red Fox,
an imprint of Random House Children's Books
A Random House Group Company

This edition published 2009

1 3 5 7 9 10 8 6 4 2

The Random House Group Limited supports the Forest Stewardship Council (FSC), the leading international forest certification organization. All our titles that are printed on Greenpeace-approved FSC-certified paper carry the FSC logo. Our paper procurement policy can be found at www.rbooks.co.uk/environment.

Set in16/20pt Bembo Schoolbook by
Falcon Oast Graphic Art Ltd

Red Fox Books are published by Random House Children's Books,
61–63 Uxbridge Road, London W5 5SA

www.**kidsatrandomhouse**.co.uk
www.**rbooks**.co.uk

Addresses for companies within The Random House Group Limited can be found at: www.randomhouse.co.uk/offices.htm

THE RANDOM HOUSE GROUP Limited Reg. No. 954009

A CIP catalogue record for this book is available from the British Library.

Printed in the UK by CPI Bookmarque, Croydon CR0 4TD

For Tilly and Robyn,
and all at the
Engine Academy!

Astrosaurs ACADEMY

needs **YOU!**

WELCOME TO THE COOLEST SCHOOL IN SPACE . . .

Most people think that dinosaurs are extinct. Most people believe that these weird and wondrous reptiles were wiped out when a massive space rock smashed into the Earth, 65 million years ago.

HA! What do *they* know? The dinosaurs were way cleverer than anyone thought . . .

This is what *really* happened: they saw that big lump of space rock coming, and when it became clear that dino-life could not survive such a terrible crash, they all took off in huge, dung-powered spaceships before it hit.

The dinosaurs set their sights on the stars and left the Earth, never to return . . .

Now, 65 million years later, both plant-eaters and meat-eaters have built massive empires in a part of space called the Jurassic Quadrant. But the carnivores are never happy unless they're causing trouble. That's why the Dinosaur Space Service needs herbivore heroes to defend the Vegetarian Sector. Such heroes have a special name. They are called ASTROSAURS.

But you can't change from a dinosaur to an astrosaur overnight. It takes years of training on the special planet of Astro

Prime in a *very* special place . . . the Astrosaurs Academy! It's a sensational space school where manic missions and incredible adventures are the only subjects! The academy's doors are always open, but only to the bravest, boldest dinosaurs . . .

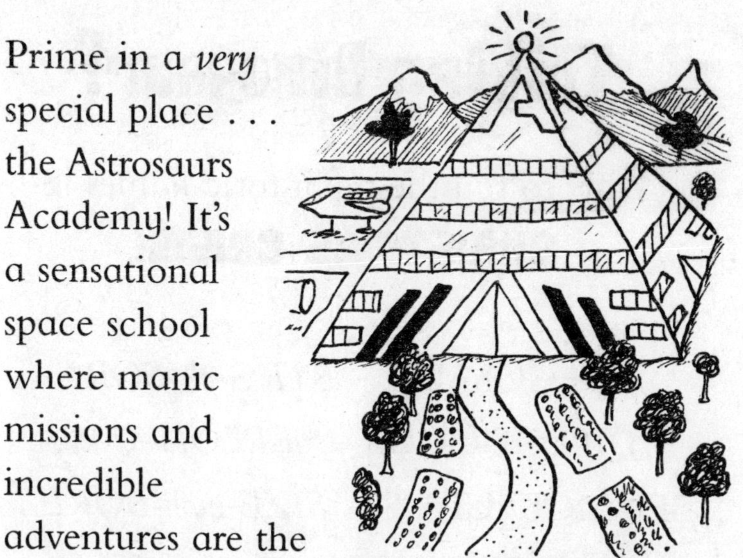

And to YOU!

NOTE: One of the most famous astrosaurs of all is Captain Teggs Stegosaur. This staggering stegosaurus is the star of many stories . . . But before he became a spaceship captain, he was a cadet at Astrosaurs Academy. These are the adventures of the young Teggs and his friends – adventures that made him the dinosaur he is today!

Talking Dinosaur!

How to say the prehistoric names in

CHRISTMAS CRISIS!

STEGOSAUR – *STEG-oh-SORE*

DIPLODOCUS – *di-PLOH-de-kus*

SEISMOSAURUS – *SIZE-moh-SORE-us*

PTERODACTYL – *teh-roh-*DAK-*til*

DICERATOPS – *dye-SERRA-tops*

DRYOSAURUS – *DRY-oh-SORE-us*

ANKYLOSAUR – *an-KILE-oh-SORE*

The cadets

THE DARING DINOS

Teggs Dutch Blink

DAMONA'S DARLINGS

Damona Netta Splatt

MAP OF ASTRO PRIME
Showing major landmarks (not to scale)
ISISSIA
Land of Wintry Wilds
CHILLICUS OCEAN
Lost Tooth Islands
Seasharp Fang
Wilderne
Moon Monitor Observatory
SALT LICK SEA
EQUATOR
Sports Village
SWETTALIA
The Stretch of Sands
Tutors' Retreat
Centre
BATTLE-SIM ZONE BETA
Mount Steamalot
VOLCALLID
Vale of Volcanoes
SPIDERIK
The Mistbou
Lava Lakes
The Pits of Flame
OCEAN OF ETERNAL

of Ice
DINO-TANK TESTING GROUND
N
W
E
S
Lakes of Strange Tonics
BACKPLATE SEA
RIK
Land
ENDODON
Land of Secrets
RELAXUS
Cadet Holiday Camp
Marine Hi-Speed Racing Course
rosaurs
ademy
Hurricane Shores
BATTLE-SIM ZONE ALPHA
The Poison Marshes
Dino Dorms
Crocodilus Sinkhole
JUNGLUS
Land of Leaves and Vines
AACUS
the World
Savage Safari Park
Fountains of Fury
SLES
Crags
Bay of Dismay
Mudlakes of Plop
AQUIS
Astro Training Pool
Wiagara Falls
SAQUARIA Land of Wet Feet
HIRLPOOLS

Chapter One

A FESTIVE CHALLENGE

There was a real feeling of Christmas in the air at Astrosaurs Academy. Snow lay all around. The tutors were walking about in red Santasaurus hats, icicles hung from every building, and bright, golden tinsel trailed from tree to tree.

Young Teggs Stegosaur smiled to himself as he trudged through the snow with his two best friends – Dutch Delaney, a dark-green diplodocus, and

a yellow dino-bird named Blink Fingawing. They were off to a special Christmas assembly in the Central Pyramid, held by Commander Gruff – the Academy's gigantic headteacher.

"I can't believe there are just two days left until Christmas Eve!" Teggs exclaimed.

Dutch nodded happily. "It'll be strange going home for a whole week's holiday."

"The holiday hasn't started yet," Blink warned him, hopping through the thick snow. "I heard one of the tutors say that old Gruff's got one extra mission for us before we go – a special challenge." He blinked excitedly. "Perhaps he's going to tell us about it now."

Dutch licked his lips. "I hope it's the kind of challenge where you have to eat five hundred puddings in under ten minutes . . ."

"Or throw a thousand snowballs in under five," Teggs added. Scooping up a lump of snow, he chucked it at Blink.

"Oh, no you don't!" With one wing, Blink whacked the snowball towards Dutch instead.

But Dutch opened his mouth and swallowed the snowball whole! "Mmmm." He licked his lips. "A grass-flavoured ice pop, delicious!"

Then he smashed his tail down into the slush and splattered Teggs *and* Blink with icy chunks! The three friends slipped and tumbled about, laughing and whooping as the snowballs flew.

"Cease-fire!" Blink called suddenly, checking his watch. "The assembly is about to start. Let's go!"

As he led the charge into the Central Pyramid, Teggs smiled. All his life he'd wanted to be an astrosaur, whizzing through space having adventures. But with friends like Blink and Dutch around, training was an amazing adventure in itself!

As they entered the crowded main hall, Teggs saw that the other first-year cadets were already there sitting in teams. And Commander Gruff was glaring at them from the stage . . .

"Well, if it isn't the Daring Dinos!" Gruff boomed. He was a grizzled, green seismosaurus, chomping on a huge stripy candy cane as though it were a cigar. "Nice of you to join us, troops! Why are you late?"

Teggs gulped. "We, er . . . we were studying the speed of frozen missiles in a close-quarters combat situation."

"If you mean you were having a snowball fight, cadet, then say so." Gruff smiled grudgingly. "Seeing as it's Christmas, I'll let you off. Now, SIT!"

Wiping their brows, the Daring Dinos dashed to their seats.

"Listen up, troops," bellowed Gruff. "Your final challenge this year is a bit of festive fun . . . But it will also test your powers of invention, your imagination and your ability to work under pressure – all essential astrosaur abilities." He surveyed the cadets, slurping on his candy cane. "Working in your usual teams, you have just twenty-four hours to come up with the most impressive, unusual, awe-inspiring Christmas decorations ever seen!"

A buzz of whispering chatter swept through the hall.

"Please, sir?" Blink asked. "Where can we find the things we need to build these decorations?"

"All over the planet," Gruff declared. "Astro-jets are waiting on the launch pads with robot pilots. You can tell them where you want to go – but to make sure you don't get into trouble, they will only fly you to *safe* locations."

Teggs turned to Dutch and sighed. "Shame!"

"Remember, troops – your decorations must be finished by tomorrow evening at six o'clock. We shall display them on the athletics track, and I will judge your efforts."

"What prize do we win?" cried a pretty red diceratops, bouncing up and down in her seat.

"Trust Damona to ask a question like that," Dutch muttered.

Teggs smiled ruefully. Damona Furst was one of the smartest, bravest and strongest cadets at the Academy. Unfortunately, she knew it!

"The winning team will receive the special Yuletide Medal." Gruff held up a silver badge shaped like a fir tree, and the crowd ooohed and ahhed.

"They will also be guests of honour at the Festive Feast tomorrow evening – where they will be served by their fellow cadets all night." Gruff grinned as the hall erupted into excited chatter. "Good luck, everyone. Disssss-MISSED!"

"Wow!" As Gruff stomped from the hall and the cadets began to plan, Damona turned eagerly to her two team-mates. "Splatt, Netta – Damona's Darlings have to win."

Splatt, a super-speedy dryosaurus, nodded so fast that his head was a blur. "Imagine wearing that lovely medal . . ."

"Imagine Teggs and his Dino Dimwits having to peel grapes for us all evening," smirked Netta, a pink ankylosaur.

"That's never going to happen," Dutch retorted.

"We'll see," said Damona, her dark eyes sparkling. "Let's get to the launch pad, team. I've just had an idea that will win us this challenge for sure."

Splatt chuckled. "I'll run on ahead and nab us the fastest spaceship . . ."

Teggs watched them go. "You've got to hand it to Damona, she's great at having ideas." He smiled grudgingly. "You can almost see the light bulbs coming on over her head."

"Damona's drippy Darlings are our biggest rivals," Dutch groaned. "If they win and we have to serve them at the feast, we'll never hear the end of it." He held out his hand, ready for a team salute. "Dudes . . . do we dare to travel the planet in search of the winning Christmas decoration?"

Blink and Teggs put their hands on his. "WE DARE!" they all shouted.

"But perhaps we don't need to travel the planet," Blink added mysteriously. "Something Teggs said has given me an amazing idea for decorations we can build right on our doorstep . . ." He somersaulted into the air and flapped madly for the door. "Come on, guys – I'll explain as we go!"

Chapter Two

BRIGHT IDEAS!

While most of the cadets followed Damona's Darlings in a mad scramble for the launch pads, Blink led Teggs and Dutch in the opposite direction towards a big, drab building.

"That's the stockroom, isn't it?" said Teggs. "Where all the Academy's supplies are kept?"

"Dullsville!" Dutch frowned. "What's going on, dude?"

Blink threw open the door and started flapping about from shelf to shelf. "Give me five minutes and I'll show you."

Teggs and Dutch shrugged and settled down to wait. Dutch pulled a packet of plants from his belt. Teggs sniffed curiously. "What are those?"

"My mum sent me some chilli leaves for the journey home on Christmas Eve," Dutch explained. "Want one?"

Teggs eagerly gulped down a leaf. Then his face turned bright red, his eyes watered and smoke started belching from his mouth!

"They're kind of hot," Dutch added with a smile. "Just the thing for keeping out the Christmas cold . . ."

Gasping and spluttering, Teggs ran over to a nearby shelf, grabbed a giant-sized bottle of swamp juice, tore off the lid and gulped down the lot!

"Ahhhhhh . . ." He wiped the sweat from his forehead and grinned at Dutch. "I think I'll *leaf* those alone in future!"

Suddenly, Blink popped up behind him – and plucked the empty juice bottle from his hand. "Just what I need!" the dino-bird declared, before hopping away.

"What *is* Blink up to?" Teggs wondered. With Dutch at his side, he followed their friend . . .

Just as a glaring, festive green light shone out from the shadows.

"*Whoa!*" Dutch shielded his eyes. "Who's there?"

"Only me!" called Blink. The light bobbed towards them – and now Teggs could see that the pterosaur was holding up the green juice bottle with a light bulb inside! It was powered by a cable that trailed out of the neck and into a nearby generator.

"So that's your plan," said Teggs, grinning. "We make our own super-sized fairy lights!"

Blink nodded eagerly. "Hundreds and hundreds of them! This storeroom is full of spare light bulbs for the dorms. I'm good at power systems so I can wire them all together."

"And I've seen loads of old juice bottles in the recycling bins," said Dutch. "We could even paint them different colours . . ."

"And hang them in the trees surrounding the athletics track," Teggs suggested.

"Imagine everyone's faces when they see those lights all around the Academy!" Dutch beamed. "I'll grab the light bulbs."

"I'll get the cables," said Blink.

"And I'll fetch the bottles and start painting them," said Teggs. "Even if we don't win it's going to be an awesome display!"

Outside on the launch pad, Damona's Darlings' astro-jet was first into the air. The large, computerized control room had been decorated with paper chains and fake snow.

"We have lift off!" said the robot pilot, a party hat perched on its head. "Where do you wish to go?"

Netta and Splatt looked expectantly at Damona.

"Well . . ." Damona smiled. "As you know, my Uncle Hiro is a famous astrosaur. And he once told me that the tallest, largest Christmas trees in the whole Jurassic Quadrant grow right here on Astro Prime. Apparently they were first discovered during Raptor War Five."

"Wow!" said Netta. "Imagine if we could bring back one of those!"

"We can," Damona told her. "These C-Class astro-jets come with a built-in anti-gravity super-winch – they can lift a thousand tons easily."

Splatt rubbed his hands together eagerly. "And where can we find these Christmas trees?"

"They grow on Endodon," said Damona. "The Land of Secrets."

"Warning!" A light on the robot pilot started flashing red. "Endodon is *not* a safe place. It has a double-alpha security rating. I cannot fly there."

"Of course you can," said Damona crossly. "Don't be such a wet machine."

"Endodon's secrets are too dangerous," the robot insisted.

Netta looked uncertain. "Maybe we should think of something else . . ."

"I already have," Damona announced. "This!" She unplugged the robot pilot. "Uncle Hiro showed me how to fly one of these. *I* will take us to Endodon."

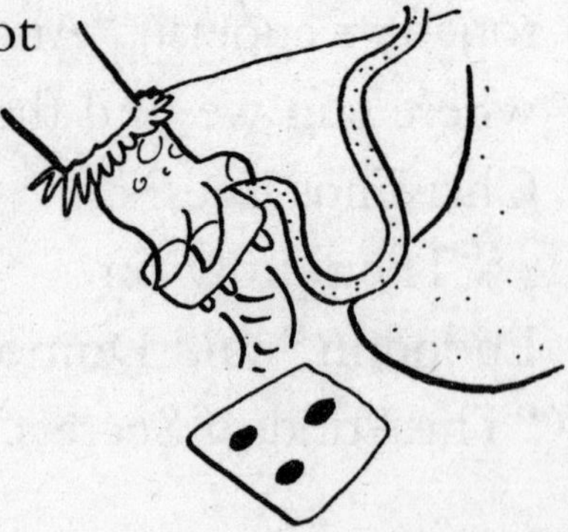

Splatt gulped. "Are you sure about this?"

"I'm sure I want to win!" Damona climbed into the pilot's seat. "The journey will only take a few hours and we won't even have to land. We'll find a tree, lift it with the super-winch and take it back to the Academy."

Netta gave Splatt a hopeful smile. "Doesn't sound too tricky."

"Relax, team!" Damona gave Splatt and Netta her most dazzling smile. "My Christmas gift to you will be winning that Yuletide Medal. What can possibly go wrong . . . ?"

Chapter Three

DAZZLING DISASTER!

In the big storeroom, the Daring Dinos spent all that night and most of the next day working on their Christmas decorations. They sang carols, ate ferns, and slurped plenty of festive pine juice. Teggs had painted hundreds of old bottles in bright and beautiful colours.

Dutch had placed a bulb in each of them, and Blink had then wired them all together.

As a finishing touch, the three friends were tying ivy and holly – freshly picked from the Academy forests – around the cables to make them look extra festive.

"All together now," cried Teggs. "*Dino-saw three ships come sailing in . . .*"

Dutch joined in tunelessly. "*On Christmas Day, on Christmas Day . . .*" He put down his holly and yawned loudly.

"You know, I haven't worked so hard in ages. I could sleep for a week."

"What, and miss Christmas?" Blink teased, tying a last piece of ivy around the tangled lead. "There! All finished!"

Teggs stretched and checked his watch. "And just in time – there's only an hour until the judging begins!"

"So what are we waiting for?" Dutch grabbed a big bunch of bulb-filled bottles. "Let's hang them up!"

The sun was slowly setting as the Daring Dinos rushed out to the ring of trees that surrounded the athletics track. Teggs and Dutch busied themselves arranging their home-made fairy lights in the snowy branches. Blink hooked up his cables to an outdoor generator in a small shed that gave power to the track's floodlights.

"Finished!" Teggs cried, shaking snow from the plates on his back just as the Academy's clock chimed quarter-to-six.

Blink turned towards the generator hut. "We'd better test that the lights actually work."

"No time, dude," Dutch whispered. "Here come the other teams."

Teggs looked over to see a parade of excited cadets tramping through the snow. They were towing huge trailers and toboggans behind them, their handiwork hidden by sheets and blankets – except for Splatt and Netta,

who hadn't brought anything. They were wearing jet-packs on their backs and smiles on their faces.

"Why do you need to fly up into the air?" Teggs asked them. "And where's Damona?"

Netta swapped a smug smile with Splatt. "You'll soon find out!"

"Get ready, troops!" Commander Gruff's voice boomed out like a foghorn. "I've brought a few friends along to help me with the judging . . ."

With a tingle in his tum, Teggs saw that Gruff was striding towards the track along with every other instructor at the Academy!

"It's time to check those decs," the commander bellowed, chomping on another giant candy cane. "Starting with the Triceratops Troop!"

Trebor, a large grey triceratops, pulled the blanket from his team's trailer to reveal a pile of giant pine cones, glowing with silver light. "We found these in Quarrik, the wilderness land," he declared. "And we found some leftover luminous paint inside the old spaceport there."

"Good exploring," growled Gruff, and the other tutors nodded.

"Now, the Baggy Brothers – what have you got?"

Ick, Wick and Honko, who were triplets, jumped up. "It's totally Chris-ma-saurus!" said Ick, pulling out a remote control.

"And then some," added Honko, yanking away the big blanket that covered the team's trailer. "We took some spare parts from the training robots over on Junglus, put them together and . . ."

Teggs gasped as Ick fiddled with the remote and ten large Christmas baubles rose up from the trailer and spun around in midair.

"Radio-controlled decorations," Wick explained. "You can hang them anywhere at the touch of a button!"

Ick hooked a bauble over the end of the commander's candy cane, and everyone laughed.

Luckily, so did Gruff! "Nice steering," he remarked, unhooking the bauble and tossing it back to Wick. "Now, who's next . . . ?"

Teggs fizzed with nerves as the other cadets were asked to present their decorations. The Leaf-Loving Squad had carved an amazing ice-statue of

Papa Claws using frozen rock from Isissia, the Ever-Ready Reptiles had made a gigantic snow globe using white sand from Swettalia . . .

It seemed to take for ever, but at long last Gruff looked down at Teggs, Blink and Dutch. "What have you got, boys?"

Teggs looked at Blink and Dutch and took a deep breath. "Here goes!"

The other cadets frowned as the Daring Dinos raced over to the generator hut and threw open the door. Blink gulped. "I hope the lights work . . ."

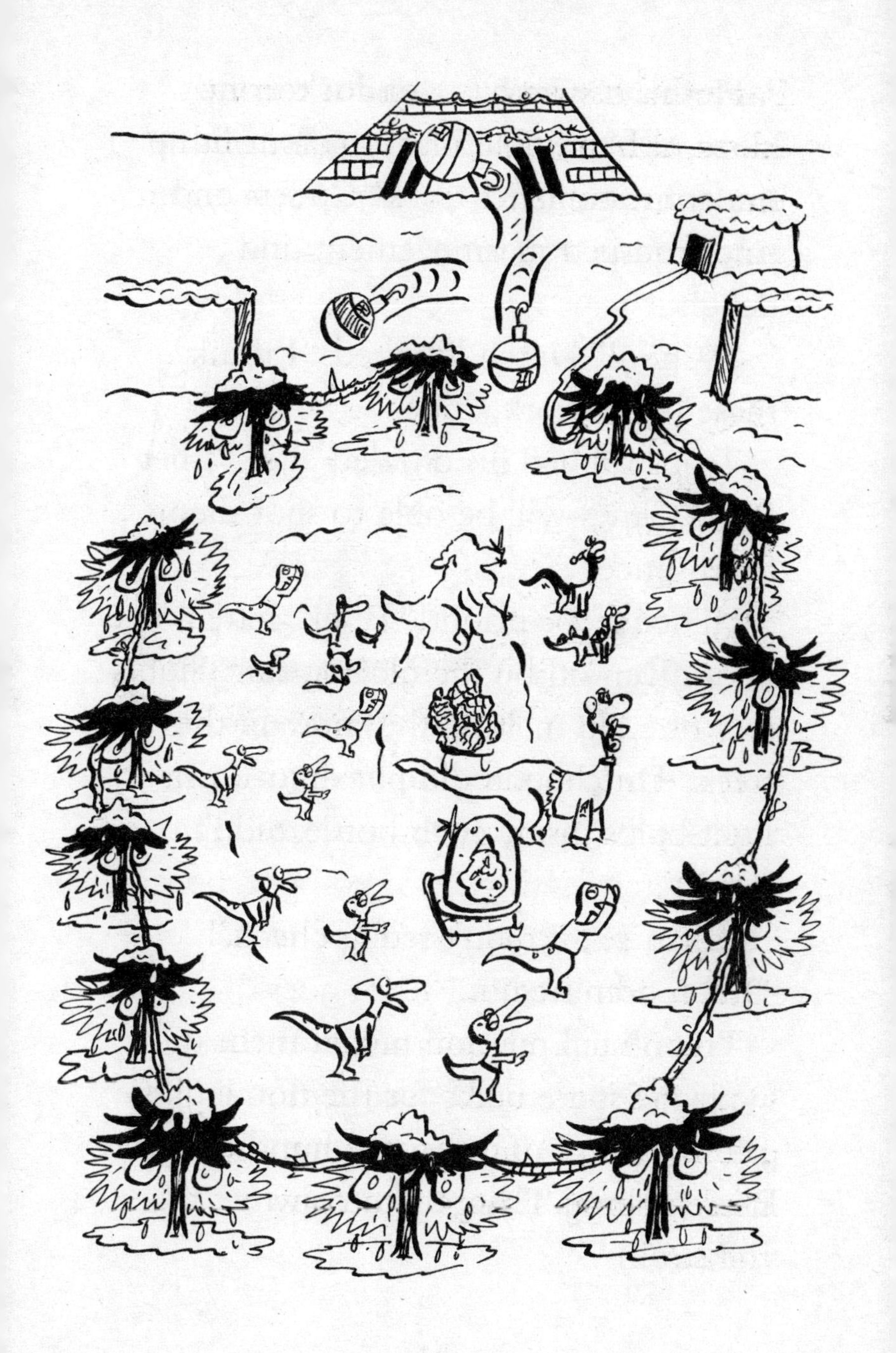

He hit a switch . . . and a terrific blaze of blindingly bright colour lit up the entire athletics track! Cadets and tutors gasped in amazement and delight.

"Whoa!" Dutch laughed. "I think these lights work, dude."

Teggs rubbed his dazzled eyes. "I bet Papa Claws will be able to spot them from space!"

"They're *too* bright!" Blink fretted. The heat given off by the glaring fairy lights was already melting the snow in the trees. "Dutch, you did put dino-dorm light bulbs inside each bottle, didn't you?"

"Erm . . . I didn't really check," Dutch admitted.

"Don't tell me you mixed them up with the spare bulbs for the floodlights!" Blink wailed. "They use a hundred times more energy. The generator won't take the strain—"

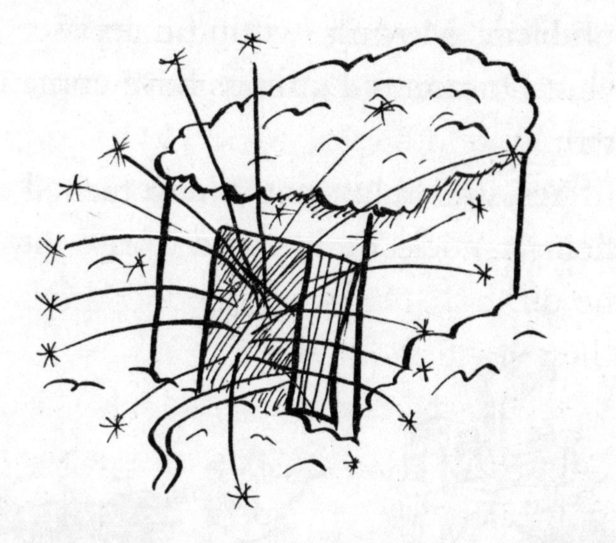

BA-BLAMMM! Sparks flew from the shed, and all the fairy lights went out.

"It will overload," Blink concluded with a sigh.

Most of the other cadets clapped politely, but Splatt and Netta started to snigger. Cheeks burning, Dutch bowed his head. "Sorry, guys."

Teggs patted his shoulder. "It was an easy mistake to make, Dutch."

The three friends walked slowly back to join their fellow cadets.

"You can fix the damage later," Gruff

rumbled. "Moving swiftly on, let's see what Damona's Darlings have come up with."

"Yes, sir!" Splatt and Netta turned on their jet-packs and started to rise into the air.

Then Splatt pulled out a communicator. "Damona? Bring the ship into position – we're ready to go!"

Teggs frowned as he heard the sound of powerful engines drawing closer. Suddenly, an astro-jet rose up into the twilight sky from behind the trees, its nose pointing towards them. It came

slowly closer, carrying something beneath it like a gigantic green arrowhead. As the astro-jet turned towards the centre of the sports track, everyone watching gasped in amazement. The green arrowhead was only the tip of a very long, super-enormous Christmas tree with a trunk as thick as the spaceship itself!

"Pretty cool, huh!" Netta yelled down at the crowd, as she and Splatt flew up to the giant tree and worked with the super-winch to slowly shift it into a standing position.

"I've seen space stations smaller than that tree!" Blink declared, and Teggs nodded in wonder.

Splatt and Netta helped steer the base of the massive trunk into the deep snow, then kept it upright with astro-clamps. Damona's voice echoed from the ship's loudspeakers: "Here we are! A great big Christmas gift from Damona's Darlings . . ."

"End of contest," Dutch sighed as the other cadets started clapping. "They've won for sure."

But over the roar of the astro-jet's engines and the cheers of the crowd, no one heard the sinister, splintering sounds from somewhere deep inside the tree. The sounds of something straining to be free . . .

Chapter Four

TREE-TRUNK TERROR

Teggs couldn't help but join in with the applause. It really was an amazing tree.

However, Commander Gruff was *not* clapping. He had turned pale, and bit down so hard on his candy cane it snapped in two. "It can't be," he muttered as the astro-jet came into land beside the tree.

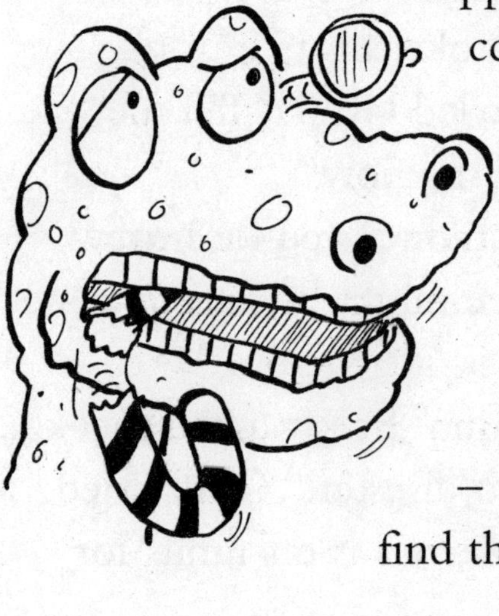

"Splatt, Netta – where did you find this thing?"

Splatt and Netta looked shifty as they shrugged off their jet-packs. "Er . . ."

Damona galloped out of the ship and saluted Gruff. "Is anything wrong, sir?"

"Just tell me you didn't overrule your astro-jet's robot pilot and that you didn't take this tree from Endodon!" growled Gruff. "Tell me clearly, and tell me now."

"Um . . ." Damona's red face grew redder. "The tree might be *slightly* from Endodon."

"Is that bad, sir?" Splatt asked meekly.

"It could be a disaster!" Gruff cried. "The Land of Secrets is off-limits for good reasons. We must take that tree away from here, right now . . ."

"Look!" called Trebor. "There's a big crack in the trunk."

"So there is." Blink hopped closer, blinking quickly. "I think there's something inside . . ."

"GET AWAY FROM THERE!" Gruff bellowed.

Blink got such a fright he flapped into the air – just as a splat of gloopy ice flew out from inside the tree trunk. It missed him by millimetres – but struck Trebor instead, right on the beak. The triceratops blinked in surprise and shook his head.

"SECURITY!" Gruff roared into his communicator. "This is a red alert. All squads report to the track, NOW!"

"Red alert?" Splatt frowned. "For a snowball?"

But Teggs could see this was no ordinary snowball. A layer of ice was forming around Trebor's nose-horn. It spread over his face and his head-frill, down his neck and across his uniform, going faster and faster . . . Within seconds, Trebor was frozen stiff and silent, sparkling like the Leaf-Loving Squad's icy statue!

"Trebor!" cried Teggs. He and Dutch rushed over to help the stricken triceratops.

"No!" Gruff whipped out his tail to hold them back. "If we can warm him up, he'll be all right, but don't touch him – or you'll turn into a living statue too!" He raised his voice. "All cadets, clear the area! Return to the main hall. NOW."

The Baggy Brothers took charge, shooing away the puzzled cadets. "You heard the boss," Ick yelled. "It's evacuate-o-saurus!"

"And then some!" Honko added.

Teggs held back with Dutch and Blink as the other cadets raced away to the Central Pyramid. "I never saw Gruff look scared before."

"Perhaps we should stick around in case we can help," said Dutch, and Blink nodded nervously.

Damona, Splatt and Netta stayed behind too, staring anxiously at poor frozen Trebor. "Oh, no . . . Sir, what have we done?"

Gruff looked grim. "You've disturbed a frosticon hive!"

"Frosticon?" Blink frowned. "I've heard that name somewhere before . . ."

"They have a double-alpha danger rating, and they hibernate in trees like this one all winter – unless they're woken early . . ." Gruff turned to his team of tutors. "The frosticons will be groggy at first. We must hold them until Security get here."

"I'll help," said Damona shakily. "I'm so sorry . . ."

"So are we," sobbed Netta.

Splatt wiped his eyes. "We'll do everything we can to put things right."

"We'll help too," Teggs declared, with Blink and Dutch beside him.

But then another sloshy ice-ball zinged out from somewhere inside the tree. It struck Colonel Oz, a space-tank tutor, right on the shoulder. Oz barely had time to gasp before he was engulfed by the spreading frost and held rigid.

"Oh, no!" gasped Netta.

"Take cover, everyone!" Gruff yelled.

Dutch grabbed hold of Teggs. "It's too far to the pyramid, and it's open ground all the way . . ."

"Let's head for the generator shed!" Teggs urged his friends.

"He's right," Damona told Netta and Splatt. "Come on!"

The dinosaurs sprinted away, apart from Blink who launched into flight.

They had barely reached the shed when a massive, creaking *CRACK* made them all turn round – just in time to see the trunk of the enormous Christmas tree burst open in a shower of splinters.

Teggs shivered as he saw a gleaming, white creature the size of a goat scuttle out from the split. He had never seen anything like it before. It looked part wolf and part scorpion, with six sparkling legs, eyes like giant ice cubes and a huge flexible stinger.

"What kind of animal is *that*?" whispered Dutch.

"I don't know," said Splatt nervously. "But I wouldn't want one as a pet!"

The weird, frosty creature arched its pointed tail over its back and swung its head from side to side. "What's all this then, eh?" it rasped in a high-pitched whisper. "Who dares to disturb the long, cold kip of Scorpo, King of the frosticons, eh? *Eh?*"

Gruff took a cautious step closer. "It was an accident," he assured the strange beast. "We mean you no harm. Please, return to your sleep."

Teggs could see Gruff's security squad – a band of burly ankylosaurs in red uniforms – creeping up on Scorpo and his humongous tree. Their stun-guns were drawn and ready.

"Just a sec, long-neck." Scorpo pointed to the decorated pyramid with one leg, his voice hardening like ice. "What's all *that*, then? Tinsel? Baubles? Can it be . . . the time of *Christmas*? Eh?"

"No! Definitely not," Gruff blustered. "It's . . . it's Easter. But, er, we didn't have the right decorations so—"

"Shut your fibbing fern-chute!" rasped Scorpo. "It *is* Christmas, I can smell it in the air! Crummy, codswallopy Christmas . . ."

"What's his problem?" Teggs frowned. "Who doesn't like Christmas?"

"And if it *is* Christmas," Scorpo went on, "that means it's time to ATTACK!" The cadets gasped as dozens more of the creepy creatures came scrabbling out of the tree trunk, haring about in all directions. "Put 'em on ice, my frosty hive-brothers!"

"Open fire!" Gruff yelled in reply.

The security squad blasted away at the frosticons, and the tutors got shooting too. But the dinosaurs were hopelessly outnumbered. The frosticons shrugged off the stun-rays and fired explosions of icy sludge from their twitching tails. Every shot seemed to find its target. Teggs stared in horror as teachers and guards alike were sloshed with the sinister slush. It soon held every one of them frozen to the spot, encased in ice.

"Oh, no!" squealed Netta. "They've even hit old Gruff!"

It was true. The seismosaurus was seizing up as glittering slush spread over his body. He turned to face Teggs and the others. "We'll be all right," he shouted over to them as his long neck frosted up. "Quick, you must get the lights . . . only chance . . . to stop them . . ."

The words froze on his lips as the eerie ice left him silent and still.

"Oh, help!" Blink clutched his beak in alarm. "Now the only real astrosaurs around here are completely helpless!"

"We're on our own." Damona blinked large, wet tears from her eyes. "And it's all my fault!"

"True," said Dutch bluntly.

"Never mind that," said Teggs. "What did Gruff mean about lights being our only chance to stop the frosticons?"

"Who knows?" cried Splatt. "We're doomed!" The others shushed him – but too late.

"What's this?" Scorpo swung round to face the shed. "More silly dinosaurs trying to hide, eh? Think we're stupid, eh?" He chuckled. "Come on, hive-brothers – this bunch look like they'd enjoy some Christmas *icing*!"

Teggs and Damona stepped forward to shield their friends, tails raised and ready to fight as a dozen frosticons came scuttling towards them . . .

Chapter Five

GIVING THE SLIP!

Teggs saw the frosticons arch their tails as they ran, ready to fire their sting-spray. *SPLAT! SPLISH!* The first two missiles came shooting towards him and he dodged aside. Damona ducked too as an ice splosh whizzed over her head.

Teggs turned to Blink, Dutch, Netta and Splatt. "Run, guys!"

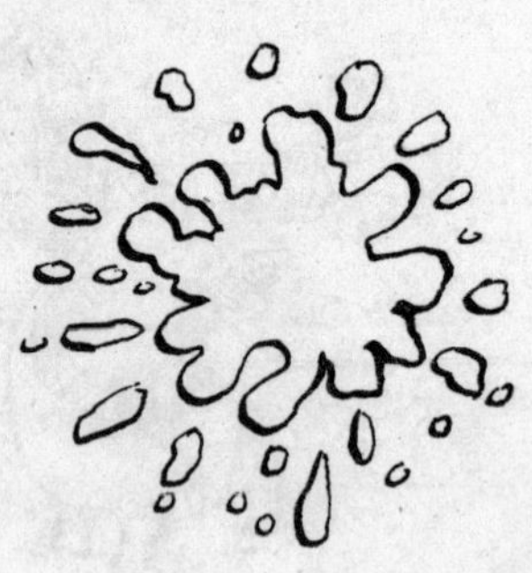

"We'll hold them off," Damona added.

"We can't leave you here!" said Blink.

"Right." Netta pushed forward to stand between Teggs and Damona. "We'll fight together."

"Prepare to freeze," hissed the nearest frosticon. It fired burst after burst of slush from its tail. Teggs avoided the first few but then slipped in the snow, a sitting target . . .

Until something large and silvery whizzed into the slush-ball's path, shielding Teggs from harm. With a gasp, he realized it was one of the Baggy Brothers' remote-controlled decorations!

"Come on, you lot!" cried Wick, busily working the remote control from behind a hastily built snow-shelter.

Teggs scrambled up as more of the gleaming baubles swished over the frosticons' heads and bashed them on their bottoms, distracting them from their attack.

"Let's go!" Dutch shouted, leading the charge towards the shelter.

"Stop them!" squealed Scorpo. He took careful aim at Netta as she ran past – but Wick sent a glittering ball hurtling into the frosticon's side, knocking him to the ground.

Splatt was first to reach Wick, narrowly beating the others. "Thanks!" he panted. "That was a fab rescue!"

"When we realised the six of you weren't in the Pyramid, we came looking," Wick explained.

"I'm glad you did!" Blink told him.

But the frosticons were targeting the baubles now, striking them again and again with splurges of ice. "The decs are getting too heavy to stay in the air!" Wick yelled. "I can't control them." He nodded towards the Central Pyramid, lit up like a big beacon in the darkening dusk. "It's time to split."

"The frosticons will outrun us on open ground," Damona panted.

Teggs pointed to the Triceratops Troop's abandoned pile of giant pine cones. "Not if we knock them off their feet!" He looked at Blink and Dutch. "Do we dare?"

"We dare!" they cried. Then the three friends charged at the pile and kicked the pine cones with all their strength. The huge seed cases rolled over and over, gathering more and more snow before smashing into the oncoming frosticons and sending them flying.

"Good job!" shouted Damona, leading Splatt, Netta and Wick away from the shelter. "Now, COME ON!"

The Daring Dinos charged after their friends and made it back to the pyramid in record time. Teggs was glad to see the other cadets had made the most of their head start. Led by Honko and Ick, they had blocked the front doors with Christmas trees from the canteen and tied tinsel tripwires to teetering stacks of desks to keep out intruders. Only a small gap in the doorway remained to allow the fleeing dinosaurs through. Once inside, Teggs and his friends huddled next to a portable heater in the entrance hall, glad for its comforting warmth.

"We thought we could use the heater to try and thaw out Trebor and the tutors," said Ick. "But I guess the frosticons would ice it up in two seconds."

"And you with it," said Splatt miserably, "thanks to us."

"All the other cadets are making the main hall as secure-a-saurus as they can," Ick reported. "Now you're here, we can finish this barricade."

Damona was already on the case. "Help me move these spare desks in front of the door," she told her team-mates, and they rushed to obey.

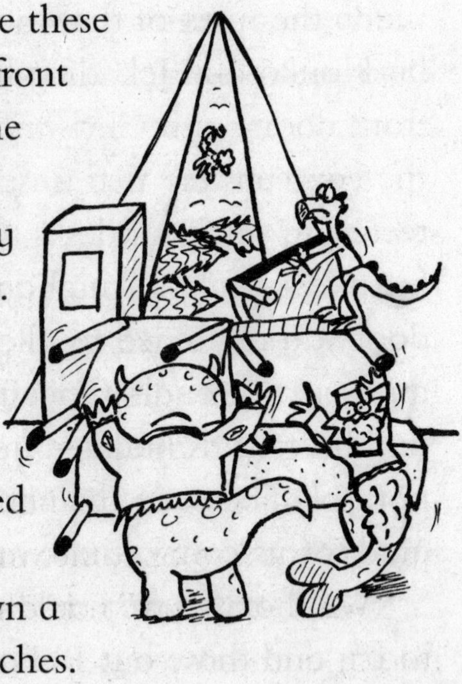

"Are there any more lights we can turn on?" puffed Teggs, quickly chomping down a couple of branches.

"According to Gruff, the frosticons don't like light."

"Maybe because they've been sleeping in the dark for ages," Netta reasoned, dragging a desk into place.

Damona sighed. "If only we knew more about those horrid things."

Splatt nodded. "Like: Why do they hate Christmas so much?"

Blink tapped his head crossly. "I'm sure I've heard of the frosticons somewhere before."

"Old Gruff certainly seemed to know all about them," said Dutch. "Maybe we should check out his office. He might have files there or something."

"Good thinking," said Teggs. "We might learn something that will help us beat them. And since it's an emergency, I'm sure he won't mind us taking a look."

"Even if we don't find anything, Gruff must have a hotline to DSS HQ. We can ask for help!" Damona charged away along the corridor. "I'll check it out."

"Hey, it was my idea," Dutch protested, hurrying after her.

"Wait for me!" Blink squawked, launching himself away.

Teggs turned to Splatt and Netta. "Why don't you collect all the lights in the pyramid and bring them back here?"

Splatt folded his arms. "And what will you be doing?"

"Staying here with the Baggy Brothers, ready to fight off the frosticons when they launch their next attack," said Teggs. "Would you like to swap?"

"Um, no." Splatt gulped. "Actually, I love collecting lamps. I'm an expert! Come on, Netta . . ."

As Splatt and Netta hurried away, Ick peered out through the barricade. "Weird-o-saurus," he murmured. "I thought the frosticons would have followed you guys straight here."

Wick pushed up beside his brother. "You mean they haven't?"

Teggs joined them, gazing out onto the wintry wonderland beyond the pyramid, bright in the glare of the security lamps. It seemed entirely deserted.

"I wonder where they went?" said Honko nervously.

Teggs felt cold, despite the warm glow of the heater. "And what are they planning to do when they get there?"

Chapter Six

POWER PLAY

Dutch, Blink and Damona hared up the stairs to the top floor of the pyramid. Commander Gruff's office was right at the pointy tip so he had plenty of room to wave his super-long neck around.

When they got there, they found the door was locked – so Damona lowered her head and charged at it, smashing it off its hinges.

Dutch frowned. "If Gruff ever thaws out, he's not going to like *that*!"

"He'll probably throw me out of the Academy in any case." Damona sighed. "It was all my idea to go to Endodon – Splatt and Netta didn't want to go. I know I broke the rules a bit, but I never dreamed that something like this could happen . . ."

Dutch patted her awkwardly on the back. "What's done is done, dude. But what made you go to Endodon in the first place?"

Damona shrugged. "My Uncle Hiro said giant Christmas trees were discovered there during Raptor War Five . . ."

"That's it!" squawked Blink, making his friends jump in the air. "I *knew* I'd heard about the frosticons before. It was in a history book – something to do with the raptors, a long, long time ago . . ." He flapped onto Gruff's desk and started pecking at a large computer keyboard. "I'll see if I can hack into the Academy files. You try to get Gruff's communicator working."

Dutch crossed to where a large bank of controls and a microphone were built into one of the walls. He pressed some buttons, but nothing happened. "The controls are locked."

"They must be password protected."

Damona groaned. "How can we find out Gruff's password?"

"I've just cracked the one on his computer," cried Blink. "It's Banana3000." He gasped. "*And* I've just found a frosticon file . . . dating from one hundred years ago!"

Dutch joined him at the computer. "What does it say?"

"*The frosticons were discovered by the raptors and used as living weapons during Raptor War Five*," Blink read aloud. "*They were naturally nasty, but the raptors made them worse – by training them to*

hate everything to do with Christmas. The slightest mention of the festive season turned the creatures into angry agents of icy destruction! They were smuggled onto Astro

Prime inside giant Christmas trees, which the raptors gave to the DSS as pretend goodwill gifts during the war's six-day cease-fire . . ."

"And I'll bet they did their best to ruin Christmas then just like they're trying now," Dutch growled.

"Hey!" Damona shouted as the bank of machinery hummed into life. "That password worked on these controls too. The communicator's starting up!"

"This is the DSS hotline operator," said a soft robotic voice. "Please state name and security code."

"I'm Damona Furst, calling from Commander Gruff's office at Astrosaurs Academy," she said urgently.

But suddenly the controls went dead. So did the lights, and Gruff's computer.

"Oh, no!" wailed Damona in the dark. "We've lost all power!"

"Or someone's *taken* it," said Dutch, peering out of the triangular window. "Look!"

Blink and Damona saw that he was pointing to the main generator room –

a boring, boxy, blue building just a few hundred metres away. A moment later, Scorpo and his fellow frosticons burst out from inside.

Dutch quietly opened the window a crack.

"Well done, hive-brothers." Scorpo's voice sliced sharply through the night. "Now we've cut the power to this entire complex, these dino-dingleberries are at our mercy . . ." He arched his stinger high over his head and reared up on his hind legs. "INVADE THE PYRAMID!"

Blink turned a panicky, extra-flappy somersault as the frosticons beetled away. "Oh, no!" he squeaked. "If only we'd had time to read to the end of that file. We still don't know how the DSS used lights to beat those things!"

"Without power, no lights will even work," Dutch reminded him.

"And now we can't call for help!" Pulling a torch from her belt, Damona ran for the door. "Well, I got us into this, so I'll just have to get us out. But first, we must warn Teggs and the others – we're under attack!"

*

No sooner had Splatt and Netta got back to Teggs, Ick and Wick with more lamps and lanterns, than the power went off! The cadets gasped as the pyramid was plunged into darkness. The only light now came from the portable dung-burner, its little flames lighting the hall with an orange glow.

"Splatt!" hissed Netta, "where is that torch you were holding . . ."

He quickly flicked it on, and a bright yellow beam cut through the gloom. "What do you think has happened?"

"Nothing good," Teggs muttered, as a wild, chittering, scuttling sound outside grew slowly louder. "And that doesn't sound like Papa Claws coming to bring us extra presents!" He grabbed the torch from Splatt and shone it through the doorway – to reveal a swarm of frosticons heading their way!

"Incoming-a-saurus!" yelled Ick.

"We'd better warn the others in the main hall," Wick realized.

"And get blocking the hall doors with another barricade," added Honko, joining his brothers as they raced away.

"We'll be back!"

Teggs noticed Splatt and Netta still hovering in the hallway. "Go with them," he urged.

"No chance," snapped Netta. "We helped cause this problem. We've got to help deal with it."

"Besides," Splatt added, "you think we're going to let you take the credit for holding off these monsters single-handed?"

"Thanks." Teggs gave them a crooked smile. "Let's just hope the tripwires slow them down . . ."

He peeped out through the doors as the invaders tripped through the ropes of tinsel, yanking piles of desks down on top of themselves.

But while a few frosticons got buried beneath them, others scrambled over the obstacles and threw themselves at the doors. Netta, Teggs and Splatt backed away on their bellies as the barricade shook and rustled, the doors inched open and ice-splats started sloshing between the desk-legs and branches.

"Not so comfy-Christmas-cosy in there now, are you, eh? Eh?" came Scorpo's sneering voice from just outside. "It's ho-ho-HOPELESS . . .

We're coming to get you!"

Desperately, Teggs jumped forward and jammed the torch through the crack in the doors, shining it right into Scorpo's face. The frosticon king shrank back for a moment, then swiped the torch from Teggs's grip. It fell to the ground, and though it kept shining up at the attacking frosticons, it didn't seem to bother them a bit.

"Light *doesn't* stop them!" Teggs shouted as the frosticons began to force their way inside. Ice-splats rained down in all directions, blocking his escape. He crawled backwards until he bumped into the portable heater, still steaming away.

Then the doors sagged open as Scorpo's hive-brothers pushed forward with all their strength. Left with no other weapons, Splatt and Netta hurled their useless lamps into the frosticons' path and took cover behind the heater.

Teggs scrambled round to join them. "So long, guys," he whispered. "It looks like this is it!"

Chapter Seven

PLANS OF PERIL

Scorpo and his army came crashing into the pyramid, their legs quivering, ribbed tails curling and uncurling . . . But then suddenly they stopped, hissing hatefully at the three cadets who peeped out from behind the heater.

"Well?" Teggs challenged them. "What are you waiting for?"

Scorpo scowled. "We . . . we simply want to hear you beg for mercy. After all, what else can you do – sing us some carols? Prick us with holly? Eh? Eh?"

"Better than that," said Damona, striding bravely into the entrance hall. "We can make you a deal."

Teggs frowned at her. "Deal? What are you on about?"

"Shh," she told him. "King Scorpo, we know you frosticons were trained by the raptors to hate Christmas and ice-up anyone who celebrates it . . ."

"The DSS defeated us and banished us to Endodon," rasped Scorpo. "Now we shall have our revenge!"

"But think about it," Damona went on. "There are only a few of us left here on Astro Prime. What are you going to do once you've frozen us all?"

Scorpo shrugged. "Don't care!"

"Well, you should," said Damona, holding up a slim cylinder. "This is the key to the astro-jet that carried you here. If you'll leave my friends alone, I will take you and all your hive-brothers away into space. You can invade other planets – *big* planets, full of dinosaurs celebrating Christmas . . ."

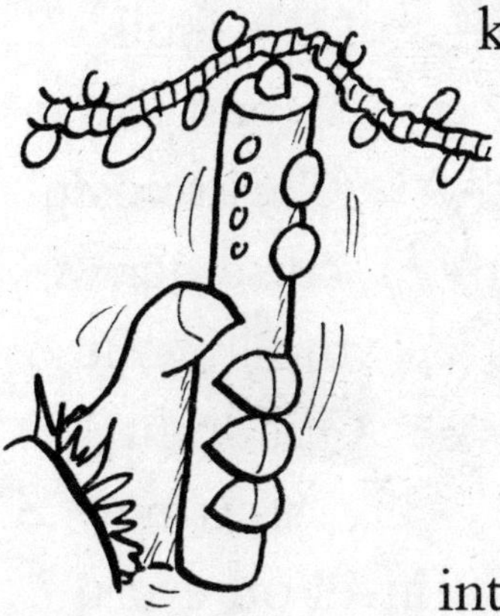

Teggs stared at her in horror. "Damona, no!"

"YES!" cried Scorpo, hopping up and down with glee. "Yes, you revoltingly rosy-cheeked, holly-berry-red dinosaur, you *shall* take us into space."

Damona nodded. "Good."

"She's gone space-crazy!" wailed Splatt. The other frosticons started to dance up and down with excitement. "We shall spread like a Christmassy curse across the Jurassic Quadrant . . . start new hives on every world . . . freeze billions of holiday-season-loving snivellers and tear their dismal decorations to tiny shreds! Eh? Eh?"

"You can't let them do this, Damona," Teggs cried.

Damona smiled at him sadly. "I have to do what's best."

Suddenly, there was a scuffle in the corridor – and Dutch hurried into sight looking very nervous. The frosticons swivelled round to face him, tails raised.

"Wait, dudes!" Dutch cried. "Uh . . . I want to help. Flying through space is hard work. Damona's got to sleep sometimes. When she does, I can take over."

Damona glared at him. Teggs opened his mouth to protest. But, unseen by the frosticons, Dutch winked at them both.

"Very well," hissed Scorpo. "Take me to your ship. But no tricks – I will leave hive-brothers on guard here until we're ready to go. Any funny business and your friends will be turned into frozen turkeys . . ."

Damona and Dutch shuffled out through the doors, closely followed by Scorpo and a horde of frosticons. But six of the creepy creatures lingered in the ruins of the barricade. Teggs, Splatt and Netta backed away cautiously and spotted Blink waiting in the shadowy corridor.

"I'm glad you're here, Blink," Teggs whispered. "What are Damona and Dutch up to?"

"Damona told us her plan on the way down," Blink said quietly. "She's tricking the frosticons. She's going to fly them straight into a black hole."

Teggs gasped. "But that means certain death for her as well as them!"

"That's why I asked Dutch to try and stop her," said Blink. "Because I think I've worked out the frosticons' weakness!"

"Well, it's certainly not light," sighed Teggs. "When I shone my torch at Scorpo, nothing happened. Gruff must have been wrong."

"No, he wasn't." Blink's eyes were shining. "He told us to 'get *the* lights'. Not just any old lights – our giant decorations!"

"But they didn't even work!" said Netta.

"For a while they did," Blink persisted. "And when a bulb burns brightly, it doesn't only give off light, does it?"

"It gives off heat too," said Teggs with growing excitement. "We saw the snow melt away as soon as the fairy lights were turned on. The frosticons' weakness isn't light at all – it's *heat*!"

"At least until they've had a chance to wake up properly," Blink agreed. "That's why they had to destroy the pyramid's main generators before they could come inside. With the central heating on, it was too warm for them."

Splatt's eyes widened. "And *that's* why Scorpo stayed in the doorway when we hid behind that portable heater."

Netta nodded. "The warmth forced the frosticons back."

"Guys," said Teggs excitedly, "somehow we've got to sneak outside, repair that generator, get our giant fairy lights working properly and use their heat to beat the frosticons. If we can't, it's curtains for us all – and for Christmas too!"

Chapter Eight

CAROLS AND CARNAGE

Suddenly, Blink started at a sound from behind them. A shadowy figure was moving further down the corridor. Teggs braced himself for action . . .

But it was only Wick. "What's happening?" the triplet asked. "We're ready to defend the main hall.

Where did the frosticons go?"

"Most of them are out in our astro-jet," said Netta, and she went on to explain what had happened with Damona and Dutch.

"Blink, Splatt, Netta and I have to get outside," Teggs told Wick. "Can you and the other cadets distract the frosticons left outside the doors?"

"Sure!" said Wick. "They'll be glad for a bit of action – and I've got an idea of what we can do. Be ready to run through the doors the moment those overgrown insects shift."

"Thanks!" Teggs hissed after him as he charged back towards the hall.

"I wonder what he has in mind," Splatt wondered nervously.

They found out just a few minutes later as the sound of rousing carols came echoing through the night.

"Wick's got everyone singing!" Netta realized. "Of course – those monsters can't stand anything to do with Christmas."

With a fierce chittering noise, the frosticons on guard duty scuttled off to investigate.

"That's our cue to get going," Teggs murmured. "Ready, guys?"

"I think so," said Blink.

"Then let's go." Teggs stuck his head out of the door – and saw that Ick and a bunch of other cadets had gathered on one of the pyramid's upper floors. They were crooning Christmas songs through the windows at the top of their lungs! Incensed, the frosticons were firing ice-blob after ice-blob at them. But the cadets kept ducking down so the missiles missed their mark.

"Time to go," Teggs told his friends. "Head straight for the generator shed – as quietly as you can."

Swiftly, the cadets slipped through the doors and out into the shivering cold of the moonlit night. They kept low to the snowy ground, which gave Teggs and Netta cold, wet bellies! The chorus of carols covered the noisy crump of the thick snow under their feet, and cheered them a little as they went.

The athletics track was still littered with the looming figures of Gruff, their tutors and poor old Trebor, all frozen where they stood like glittering waxworks. It was an eerie scene.

As he crept past the astro-jet, Teggs wondered how Dutch and Damona were doing. Would the cadets finish the night as free dinosaurs – or would they be turned into living ice statues for all the Christmases to come?

On board the freezing jet, Dutch was desperately wishing he was someplace else. The air-conditioning was on full blast, and Scorpo was clattering about, flexing his stinger and almost drooling over the controls. His hive-brothers kept hissing and whispering in similar excitement.

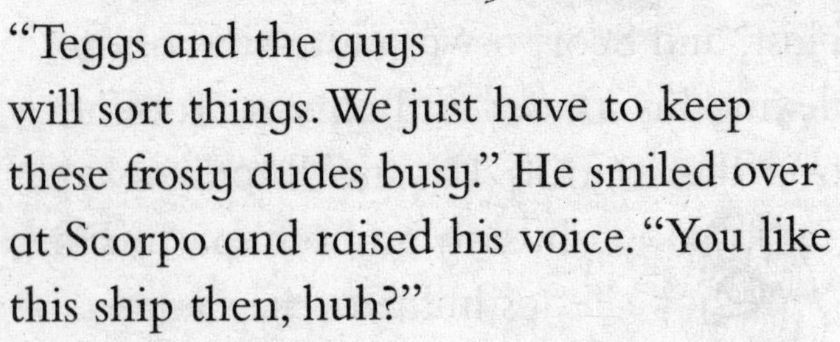

"You shouldn't have come with me, Dutch," Damona said quietly. "There's no sense in us both giving up our lives."

"I'm not giving up anything!" Dutch retorted. "Teggs and the guys will sort things. We just have to keep these frosty dudes busy." He smiled over at Scorpo and raised his voice. "You like this ship then, huh?"

"I love it!" rasped Scorpo. "My poor hive has been stuck in one place for so many years. But now . . ." He chuckled. "How long before we can lift off, eh? Eh? How long before we reach the nearest big planet full of festive fools celebrating Christmas, and spoil all their fun, eh? Eh? EH?"

Damona looked nervously at Dutch. "Um . . . I just need to do some pre-flight checks."

"Remember, no tricks," Scorpo hissed. "Or I'll put you and your friends on ice in a trice!"

"Absolutely. No tricks." Dutch turned to Damona and lowered his voice. "But I sure hope Teggs has a couple up his sleeve . . ."

Outside in the generator shed, Blink was busily working. Netta kept watch for frosticons while Teggs and Splatt pulled down the enormous home-made fairy lights from the trees around the track.

"I hope Blink can get the generator

going," said Splatt from behind a huge tangle of wires and juice bottles.

But suddenly – *Brk-Brk-Brk! GRRRRR! SKEEEEEEEEE!* A terrible clanking and rumbling noise started up from the generator shed.

"Uh-oh," said Teggs, unhooking the last of the lights. "Carols won't cover that racket!"

Weighed down by the decorations, the panting pair raced over to join Netta in the shed doorway. "Blink!" she yelled. "What's going on?"

Blink was flapping about inside, all a-twitter. "I've had to rewire the generator coils," he yelled over the racket. "But the connections aren't holding properly. The power's not getting through."

"But . . ." Netta gulped. "No power means no lights . . ."

Splatt nodded. "And no lights means no heat . . ."

"And no heat means very, very bad," said Teggs, pointing grimly towards the pyramid. "Because here come the frosticons!"

Six sinister shapes were scuttling over the snow towards them at alarming speed. Teggs pushed Netta and Splatt into the shed, followed them inside and slammed the door shut.

“That won’t keep the frosticons out for more than a minute,” Splatt wailed. Already, the wooden door was shaking under the impact of balls of icy gloop.

“I can’t get this stupid generator working!” Blink moaned.

“But you must!” Teggs yelled, as a frosticon stinger came stabbing through the door. “If you don’t, it’s the end for us all!”

Chapter Nine

LET THERE BE LIGHTS!

Teggs stared, and Netta and Splatt clung to each other in terror as the door cracked open. The frosticons started to squeeze inside, all set to get the cadets . . .

And then suddenly, the generator's clunks and splutters changed to a deep and steady hum, and the fairy lights gave off a dazzling, blinding glow! The frosticons screeched and backed away in alarm as the temperature rose in seconds.

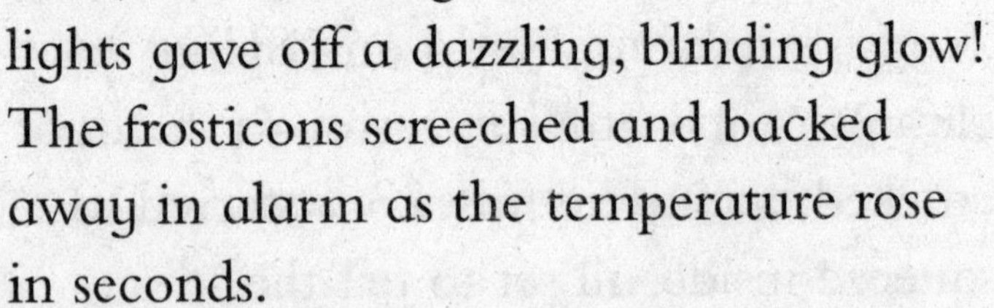

"Blink!" Teggs cheered, shielding his eyes. "You did it!"

"Way to go, beak-features!" cried Netta, as she and Splatt grabbed him in a hug.

"That was close," Blink admitted, blinking madly. "But now we must chase after those frosticons before they hurt any more of our friends!"

The four cadets carefully picked up the blazing lights and peered outside. The frosticons were retreating towards the astro-jet. They still seemed weak from the wave of unexpected heat – but two of them fired their sting-sprays.

"No, you don't," growled Teggs, dodging an ice-ball just in time. "Guys, let's get them surrounded!" He and his friends formed a circle around the frosticons. The creatures snarled and snapped as they cowered away from the heat of the lights.

"That's six of them under control," said Splatt. "But what about Scorpo and all the others?"

Even as he spoke, the doors to the astro-jet opened and Scorpo stepped outside with a handful of hive-brothers.

"What is the meaning of this disgusting festive display? Eh?" He clapped two legs together and Dutch and Damona were dragged to the doorway by two more frosticons. "Put out those lights and let my hive-brothers go – or we'll squish your friends!"

"Don't listen to him, Teggs!" Damona shouted. "He needs us to fly the ship."

"I don't," the king sneered. "Now I've watched you pressing those controls, I'll soon learn to fly it myself."

Dutch cleared his throat. "Well, if it's game over for us, dude, how about a last meal before we go?" He reached into his pocket and stuffed a handful of leaves into his mouth. Then he shoved several more into Damona's beak. She squeaked and spluttered in surprise.

Teggs gasped and grinned. "Those look to me a whole lot like—"

"Chilli leaves!" Dutch roared. His cheeks grew red, his eyes watered and he pushed out a hot, chilli-drenched breath all over Scorpo.

For the frosticon king it was like a steam pipe had burst

open in his face. "Noooooo!" he wailed, gasping and shivering. At the same moment, Damona breathed hard on his hive-brothers and drove them back inside the astro-jet. Dutch slammed the door shut with his tail, locked it, grabbed Damona and ran!

Teggs hopped up and down as his two friends raced over. "You were brilliant!"

"I was, wasn't I?" Damona agreed.

"And Dutch wasn't bad either," said Netta, kissing his cheek – which glowed even redder!

"Guys, what's happening?" called Wick.

Teggs saw that he and the other cadets had ventured out of the Central Pyramid. "When those guards stopped trying to splat us and chased after you, we were so worried . . ."

"And so you should be!" Scorpo snarled. "Now we shall freeze you all. No mercy! No second chances! No more 'Happy Christmases' for any of you ever again!"

"Oh, no!" Blink yelled, as Scorpo opened the astro-jet's doors and the frosticons swarmed out to attack.

"I think it's time we gave our captives the push!" Teggs yelled. He broke the circle of fairy lights around the six dazed frosticons and then he and Netta shoved them into their approaching hive brothers – causing a frosticon pile-up. "Quickly, everyone!" Teggs shouted to the other cadets. "We must make a ring of fairy lights around those monsters to stop them getting away. Do we dare?"

The answering cry went up: "WE DARE!" Ick, Wick and Honko led the charge of whooping cadets. Super-fast Splatt ran to meet them halfway with one end of the dazzling string of lanterns. In a matter of seconds, before the frosticons had time to untangle themselves, the cadets had them surrounded.

"Not the heat!" the frosticons wailed, shrinking away from the burning bright bulbs and the warmth they gave off as the circle of friends closed in. "Not the horrible heat!"

"Now, let's force them back inside their oversized tree," cried Dutch. The cadets cheered and started jostling the weakened frosticons towards the enormous evergreen.

"You can't do this to me!" Scorpo cried feebly. "I won't be beaten!"

"Wrong, Scorpo." Teggs stepped aside with his glowing lamp, leaving a clear pathway through the snow to the massive split in the giant tree's trunk. "It's time for you and your little helpers to vanish back up the chimney. Merry Christmas!"

"*Ugh!*" said Scorpo. "Stop it."

"Yes, Happy Christmas!" called Netta. "And a Happy New Year!"

The other cadets took up the well wishing. The cries of Christmas cheer rose into the night.

"Shut up!" Scorpo howled. "I can't bear it . . . I'm going back to sleep. Come on, lads!" He skittered away inside the tree and his hive-brothers followed feebly.

"We haven't won yet," Teggs warned his friends. "We must cover the whole tree with these lights, so the frosticons can't break out again."

"Netta and I can take care of that," said Splatt breathlessly. He pounced on two small metal bundles in the snow close by and held them up. "Ta-daaa!"

"Our jet-packs!" Netta beamed. "They helped us bring the tree here – now they can help us get rid of it."

Splatt and Netta strapped on the jet-packs and whizzed up into the air, holding the thick snaking rope of lights between them. Carefully they began to wrap them around the tree.

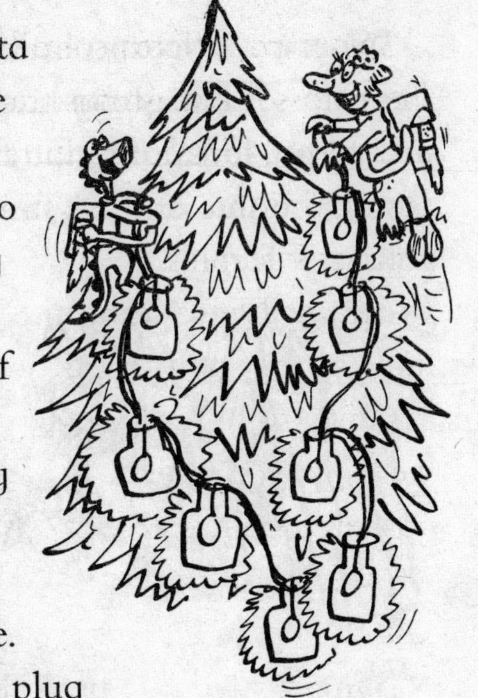

"We need to plug up that hole in the trunk too," Blink realized.

"The Triceratops Troop's luminous pine cones will do the job," said Damona racing off to grab a couple.

Teggs nodded approvingly as Dutch helped her to shove them in place. "Trebor was the first to be slushed by the frosticons – but he's still helped to save the day!"

Splatt and Netta spiralled around the colossal Christmas tree faster and faster, arranging the fiercely glowing lights in the branches at regular intervals.

And as Netta hung the last light at the very top, a massive whoop of joy went up from the gathered cadets.

"We did it!" Dutch cheered.

Blink turned an excited somersault. "The frosticons are back

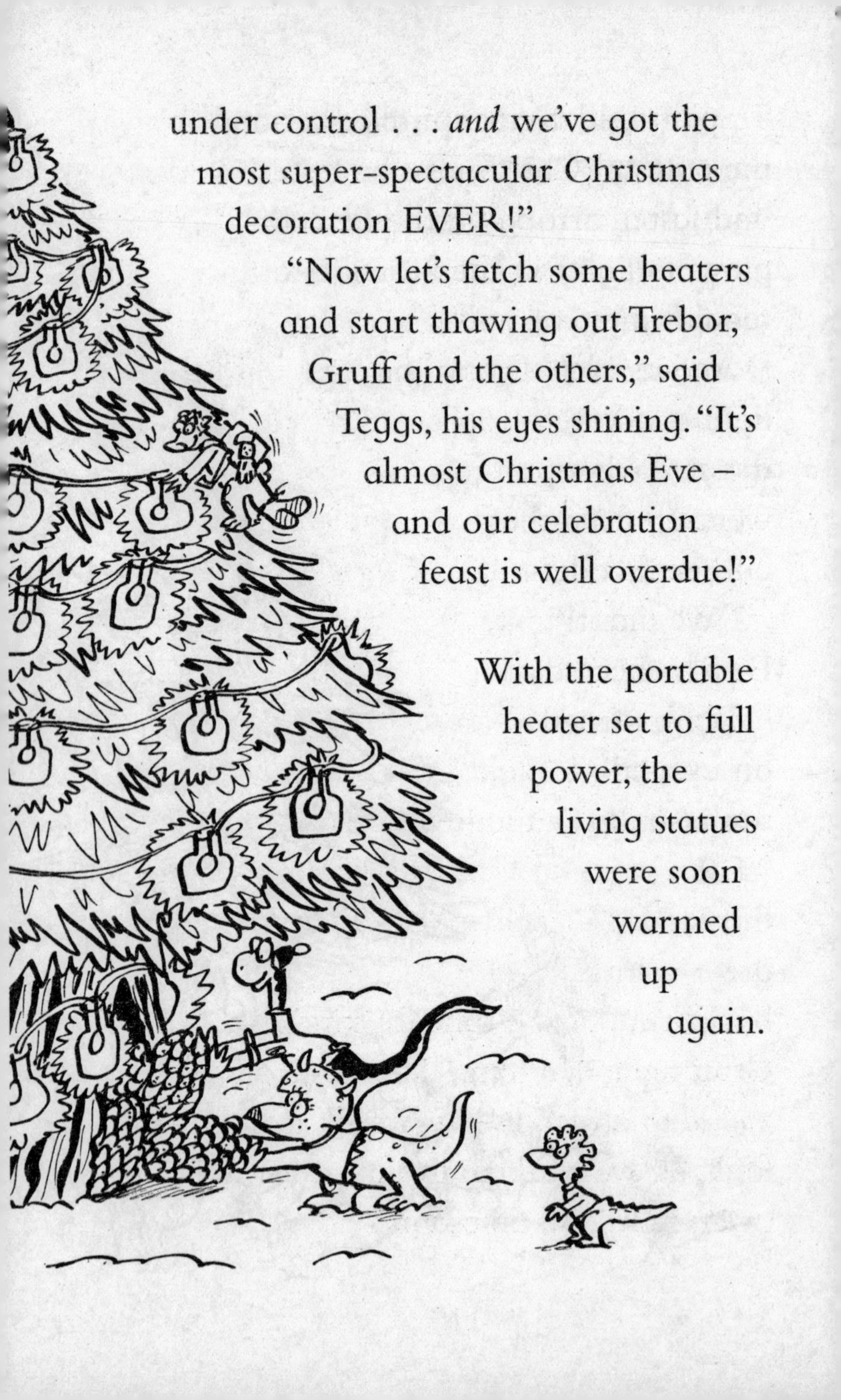

under control . . . *and* we've got the most super-spectacular Christmas decoration EVER!"

"Now let's fetch some heaters and start thawing out Trebor, Gruff and the others," said Teggs, his eyes shining. "It's almost Christmas Eve – and our celebration feast is well overdue!"

With the portable heater set to full power, the living statues were soon warmed up again.

Trebor was wrapped in blankets by his happy team-mates, Blink went to work with a battery-powered hairdryer, providing extra heat for the taller tutors, and Damona and Netta draped a large, deflated tent over Commander Gruff.

"Seems I missed all the excitement," Gruff growled, once he'd woken up. "We haven't had to fight frosticons in a hundred years."

"Yucky things!" Splatt shivered. "Why did the DSS let them stay living on Astro Prime?"

"Christmas is a time for kindness," Gruff reminded him. "The frosticons were *trained* to attack us – it wasn't really their fault. So we let them live in peace well away from any dinosaurs."

"And now we can use the astro-jet's super-winch to lift up their tree and carry them back to Endodon," said Damona, "where they can't cause any more trouble."

"And what about the trouble YOU caused by overriding the robot in the first place?" Gruff boomed.

Damona hung her head, and Splatt and Netta sighed.

"Please, sir," said Teggs. "Damona was willing to give her life to put things right. It was the bravest thing I've ever seen."

"She's a pain in the neck," said Dutch with a smile. "But I guess she's pretty cool."

"Thanks." Damona frowned. "I think!"

Blink flapped over. "What's more, we'd never have beaten the frosticons without Splatt and Netta's help."

Damona's Darlings beamed at him.

"Everyone makes mistakes," Gruff said quietly. "It's how we put things right that counts." He smiled. "You know, some day I might just make proper astrosaurs out of you all!"

"Not if we starve to death first, sir," said Teggs cheekily.

"Ah, yes. That little matter of the festive feast . . . I'll get onto it right away." Gruff stretched out his long neck. "But first, I would like to thank all you cadets for saving the Academy – and Christmas itself –

from a full-on frosty disaster! I will be awarding the special Yuletide Medal to every single one of you for top teamwork and extreme bravery."

An enormous cheer went up from the gathered cadets, just as the Academy clock chimed midnight.

"Hey, it's Christmas Eve!" Dutch declared.

Splatt jumped into a disco pose. "Let's stay up all night, feasting till the space-bus comes to take us home!"

"Sounds like a plan to me," Teggs agreed.

"And since I caused all the trouble," said Damona, "*I* will bring everyone their food and drink!"

Another cheer went up from the crowd.

"Well, I'd better get cooking in the

canteen," said Gruff, striding away. "Merry Christmas, everyone . . ."

Teggs wiped his brow. "It's certainly been a Christmas to remember!"

"Let's sing some carols," Netta suggested.

Dutch nodded. "How about 'The 'Olly and the Hivey'?"

"NO!" shouted everyone.

"How about we just look ahead to a super-exciting, mega-action-packed new year?" Teggs beamed round at his friends. "After all, here at Astrosaurs Academy, it couldn't be anything else. HAPPY CHRISTMAS!"

THE END

The cadets of Astrosaurs Academy will return in VOLCANO INVADERS!